Reading Aloud with Your Child

Research shows that reading books aloud is the single most valuable support parents can provide in helping children learn to read.

- Be a ham! The more enthusiasm you display, the more your child will enjoy the book.
- Run your finger underneath the words as you read to signal that the print carries the story.
- Leave time for examining the illustrations more closely; encourage your child to find things in the pictures.
- Invite your youngster to join in whenever there's a repeated phrase in the text.
- Link up events in the book with similar events in your child's life.
- If your child asks a question, stop and answer it. The book can be a means to learning more about your child's thoughts.

Listening to Your Child Read Aloud

The support of your attention and praise is absolutely crucial to your child's continuing efforts to learn to read.

- If your child is learning to read and asks for a word, give it immediately so that the meaning of the story is not interrupted. DO NOT ask your child to sound out the word.
- On the other hand, if your child initiates the act of sounding out, don't intervene.
- If your child is reading along and makes what is called a miscue, listen for the sense of the miscue. If the word "road" is substituted for the word "street," for instance, no meaning is lost. Don't stop the reading for a correction.
- If the miscue makes no sense (for example, "horse" for "house"), ask your child to reread the sentence because you're not sure you understand what's just been read.
- Above all else, enjoy your child's growing command of print and make sure you give lots of praise. *You are your child's first teacher — and the most important one. Praise from you is critical for further risk-taking and learning.*

— Priscilla Lynch
Ph.D., New York University
Educational Consultant

ISBN 0-590-54085-8

The Baby-sitters Club Movie © 1995 Beacon Communications Corp.
and Columbia Pictures Industries, Inc.
Text copyright © 1995 by Scholastic Inc.
Photographs copyright © 1995 by Beacon Communications Corp.
and Columbia Pictures Industries, Inc.
All rights reserved. Published by Scholastic Inc.
THE BABYSITTERS CLUB is a registered trademark of Scholastic Inc.
HELLO READER!, CARTWHEEL BOOKS, and the CARTWHEEL BOOKS logo
are registered trademarks of Scholastic Inc.

12 11 10 9 8 7 6 5 4 3 2 1   5 6 7 8 9/9 0/0

Printed in the U.S.A.   23

First Scholastic printing, August 1995

Adapted by Teddy Slater Margulies
From THE BABY-SITTERS CLUB MOVIE
Based on the best-selling series
by Ann M. Martin

Hello Reader! — Level 3

SCHOLASTIC INC. Cartwheel ·B·O·O·K·S·®
New York Toronto London Auckland Sydney

Chapter One

Kristy Has a Great Idea

It was the last week of June. School had just ended. The members of the Baby-sitters Club wondered how they would spend their summer vacation.

Kristy called their meeting to order. "I have a great idea!" she said.

The other girls smiled. They knew something good was coming. After all, it was Kristy who had thought up the Baby-sitters Club in the first place.

"Let's run a day camp this summer," Kristy went on. "It will be lots of fun. And we'll make lots of money."

Claudia was a pretty girl with long black hair. "We sure know plenty of little kids," she said. "But where would we put them all?"

There was a lot of land around Dawn and Mary Anne's house. "It would be great for a day camp," said Mary Anne.

Mary Anne and Dawn's parents agreed to let the Baby-sitters Club use their yard. On one condition . . .

"I promised we would keep the campers outside," Mary Anne said. "My dad doesn't want a bunch of children running in and out of the house all day."

"No problem," the girls said.

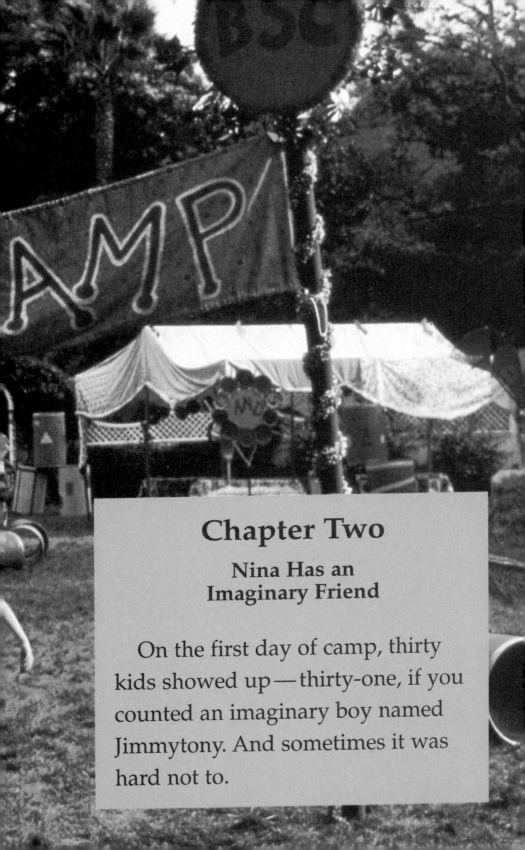

Chapter Two

Nina Has an Imaginary Friend

On the first day of camp, thirty kids showed up—thirty-one, if you counted an imaginary boy named Jimmytony. And sometimes it was hard not to.

Kristy grouped all the campers by age. Then she held up some pot holders. There were red ones and blue ones, yellow ones and green ones.

"These match your counselors' pot holders," Kristy explained. "Pin them on, and everybody will know which group you belong to."

Dawn handed four-year-old Nina a red pot holder and said, "You are going to be in my group."

Nina smiled at Dawn. Then she smiled at the empty space beside her.

"Can I have one for my friend Jimmytony?" Nina asked Dawn.

Dawn looked at the empty space and shrugged. "How old is Jimmytony?" she asked.

"The same as me," Nina said.

Dawn thought for just a moment. Then she reached out and pinned an imaginary red pot holder on the imaginary shirt of Nina's imaginary friend.

"I think I'm going to like this camp," Nina said happily.

Chapter Three

Jonas Has a Potty Problem

Later that morning, Kristy's kids were having a three-legged race. It looked as if Jonas and Nicky were going to win. They had almost reached the finish line.

Suddenly, Jonas stopped in his tracks.

Nicky tumbled to the ground.

"Jonas, why did you stop like that?" Kristy asked.

"I have to go to the bathroom," Jonas answered.

"Bathroom?" Kristy asked. "Stacey, where are those Porta Potties we ordered?"

"I don't know," Stacey said. "The man promised they would be here at eight o'clock this morning."

"Well, they're not here," Kristy said.

"I have to go!" Jonas repeated. "NOW!"

"Me too," Nicky announced.

"We have to go!" a whole chorus of voices joined in.

Matt, who was a deaf child, said it in sign language.

Jessi, Mallory, and Dawn looked worried.

"What are we going to do?" Mary Anne wailed.

"We'll have to use your house," Kristy replied.

"We can't," Mary Anne said. "We promised our parents."

Kristy looked at the girls and boys hopping up and down around her.

"I don't think we have a choice," she said. "They really have to go."

And so they went.

Chapter Four

Mrs. Haberman Has
a Lot of Patience

A very nice woman lived next door to Dawn and Mary Anne's house. Her name was Mrs. Haberman.

Mrs. Haberman loved birds and butterflies. She loved trees and flowers. She also loved little kids — until the Baby-sitters Club day camp moved in.

During the first week of camp, Jonas,
Nicky, Daniel, and Emmy made a slingshot.

They loaded it with jelly doughnuts...
and sent them flying over the hedge.

THWACK!

A big glob of red jelly landed on
Mrs. Haberman's favorite bird feeders.

Mrs. Haberman glared at the
campers and shook her head. Then she
cleaned up the mess.

Two weeks later, the same children shot a stink bomb over the hedge.

PHEW!

The smelly bomb landed right in Mrs. Haberman's garden.

Mrs. Haberman scowled at the campers and muttered something under her breath.

Mrs. Haberman had to speak up.

"I didn't complain when the children bothered my birds," Mrs. Haberman told the girls in the Baby-sitters Club. "And I didn't complain when they bothered me. But this is too much!"

"I'm so sorry," Dawn said. "I know we haven't been very good neighbors. But camp will be over soon. Can't you please put up with us until then?"

Mrs. Haberman smiled at Dawn. She really was a nice woman.

"I guess I can manage for another week or two," Mrs. Haberman said. "If you can keep your campers out of mischief until then," she added.

"We can," Dawn said. "We will!"

There were no more problems for the rest of the summer.

On the last day of camp, Dawn and her friends and all the campers went next door to say good-bye to Mrs. Haberman.

They didn't go empty-handed. They brought wagons filled with flowers for her garden.

The next day, the girls in the Baby-sitters Club figured out how much money they had earned.

Counting everything they had spent
on Porta Potties, arts-and-crafts
supplies, milk and cookies, and
Mrs. Haberman's plants, they were
left with a grand total of $18.63. They
spent it on a pizza.

"We may not have made a lot of money, but we sure had a lot of fun," Kristy said.

"And that's what it's all about. Friendship and fun!"